Prayers from the

Lorraine Gaird

Prayers from the Ark

Selected Poems by
CARMEN BERNOS DE GASZTOLD

Translated from the French by
RUMER GODDEN

Illustrated by Barry Moser

VIKING

Foreword

PRAYERS FROM THE ARK has had what could be called a hidden life, being published by the Editions du Cloitre, the private press of the Benedictine Abbaye Saint Louis de Temple at Limon-par-Igny, France, where the poet used to live and work.

I came upon the prayers by accident and was instantly caught by their charm, but do not be alarmed; the charm has nothing to do with whimsy: Carmen de Gasztold has seen too much of the seamy side of life to be a sentimental animal lover—ironically, she has little use for pets. In her world a dog is to guard the house, a horse to work its strength out for its master, a pig to be eaten, and there is an economy and sense about her work that is typically French; it is the truthfulness of the prayers, especially as it reflects on us, unthinking humans, that causes pain.

These poems are prayers, Catholic in origin but catholic also in the sense that they are for everyone, no matter of what creed. Carmen Bernos lives now in an atmosphere of prayer—and more importantly, of belief—but the poems have not been influenced by the Abbaye. Most of the prayers were written long before she came to the Abbaye, in a scant, hard time—a time of enemy occupation, hunger, cold, frustration; yet it was during this time that she was able to find, in each of these workaday, infinitesimal, or unfavored creatures, not only its intrinsic being but an unexpected grain of incense that wafts it up, consecrates it, and this in the most matter-of-fact way.

The Abbaye has only endorsed what she knew a prayer must be, if it is to have any meaning: not something dreamy or wishful, not a cry to be used in emergency, not even a plea, and not necessarily comforting. A prayer is a giving out, an offering, compounded of honest work and acceptance of the shape in which one has been created—even if it is to be regretted as much as the monkey's—of these humble things added to the great three: faith, hope, and love.

—R.G.

Noah's Prayer

ORD,
what a menagerie!
Between Your downpour and these animal cries
one cannot hear oneself think!
The days are long,
Lord.
All this water makes my heart sink.
When will the ground cease to rock under my feet?
The days are long.
Master Raven has not come back.
Here is Your dove.
Will she find us a twig of hope?
The days are long,
Lord.
Guide Your Ark to safety,
some zenith of rest,
where we can escape at last
from this brute slavery.
The days are long,
Lord.
Lead me until I reach the shore of Your covenant.

Amen

The Prayer of the Cock

Do not forget, Lord,
it is I who make the sun rise.
I am Your servant
but, with the dignity of my calling,
I need some glitter and ostentation.
Noblesse oblige . . .
All the same,
I am Your servant,
only . . . do not forget, Lord,
I make the sun rise.

Amen

The Prayer of the Dog

ORD,
I keep watch!
If I am not here
who will guard their house?
Watch over their sheep?
Be faithful?
No one but You and I
understand
what faithfulness is.
They call me, "Good dog! Nice dog!"
Words . . .
I take their pats
and the old bones they throw me
and I seem pleased.
They really believe they make me happy.
I take kicks too
when they come my way.
None of that matters.
I keep watch!
Lord,
do not let me die
until, for them,
all danger is driven away.

Amen

The Prayer of the Little Pig

LORD,
their politeness makes me laugh!
Yes, I grunt!
Grunt and snuffle!
I grunt because I grunt
and snuffle
because I cannot do anything else!
All the same, I am not going to thank them
for fattening me up to make bacon.
Why did You make me so tender?
What a fate!
Lord,
teach me how to say

Amen

The Prayer of the Donkey

 GOD, who made me
to trudge along the road
always,
to carry heavy loads
always,
and to be beaten
always!
Give me great courage and gentleness.
One day let somebody understand me—
that I may no longer want to weep
because I can never say what I mean
and they make fun of me.
Let me find a juicy thistle—
and make them give me time to pick it.
And, Lord, one day, let me find again
my little brother of the Christmas crib.

Amen

The Prayer of the Monkey

EAR God,
why have You made me so ugly?
With this ridiculous face,
grimaces seem asked for!
Shall I always be
the clown of Your creation?
Oh, who will lift this melancholy from my heart?
Could You not, one day,
let someone take me seriously,
Lord?

Amen

The Prayer of the Owl

UST and ashes!
Lord,
I am nothing but dust and ashes,
except for these two riding lights
that blink gently in the night,
color of moons,
and hung on the hook of my beak.
It is not, Lord, that I hate Your light.
I wail because I cannot understand it,
enemy of the creatures of darkness
who pillage Your crops.
My hoo-hoo-hooooo
startles a depth of tears in every heart.
Dear God,
one day,
will it wake Your pity?

Amen

The Prayer of the Cat

ORD,
I am the cat.
It is not, exactly, that I have something to ask of You!
No—
I ask nothing of anyone—
but,
if You have by some chance, in some celestial barn,
a little white mouse,
or a saucer of milk,
I know someone who would relish them.
Wouldn't You like someday
to put a curse on the whole race of dogs?
If so I should say,

Amen

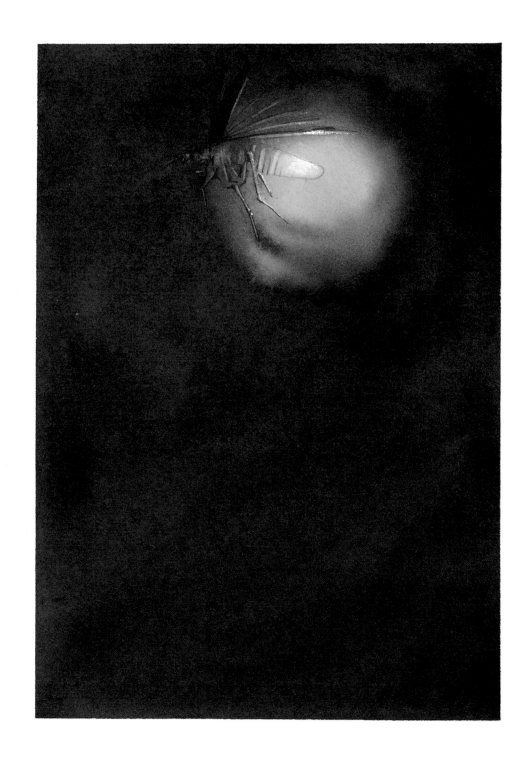

The Prayer of the Glow-worm

EAR God,
would You take Your light
a little farther away
from me?
I am like a morsel
of cinder
and need Your night
for my heart to dare
to flicker out its feeble star:
its hope, to give to other hearts,
what can be stolen from all poverty—
a gleam of joy.

Amen

The Prayer of the Goat

ORD,
let me live as I will!
I need a little wild freedom,
a little giddiness of heart,
the strange taste of unknown flowers.
For whom else are Your mountains?
Your snow wind? These springs?
The sheep do not understand.
They graze and graze,
all of them, and always in the same direction,
and then eternally
chew the cud of their insipid routine.
But I—I love to bound to the heart of all
Your marvels,
leap Your chasms,
and, my mouth stuffed with intoxicating grasses,
quiver with an adventurer's delight
on the summit of the world!

Amen

The Prayer of the Elephant

EAR God,
it is I, the elephant,
Your creature,
who is talking to You.
I am so embarrassed by my great self,
and truly it is not my fault
if I spoil Your jungle a little with my big feet.
Let me be careful and behave wisely,
always keeping my dignity and poise.
Give me such philosophic thoughts
that I can rejoice everywhere I go
in the lovable oddity of things.

Amen

The Prayer of the Ox

EAR God, give me time.
Men are always so driven!
Make them understand that I can never hurry.
Give me time to eat.
Give me time to plod.
Give me time to sleep.
Give me time to think.

Amen

The Prayer of the Dove

THE Ark waits,
Lord,
the Ark waits on Your will,
and the sign of Your peace.
I am the dove,
simple
as the sweetness that comes from You.
The Ark waits,
Lord;
it has endured.
Let me carry it
a sprig of hope and joy,
and put, at the heart of its forsakenness,
this, in which Your love clothes me,
Grace immaculate.

Amen

VIKING
Published by the Penguin Group
Penguin Books USA Inc.,
375 Hudson Street, New York, New York 10014, U.S.A.
Penguin Books Ltd, 27 Wrights Lane, London W8 5TZ, England
Penguin Books Australia Ltd, Ringwood, Victoria, Australia
Penguin Books Canada Ltd, 10 Alcorn Avenue, Toronto, Ontario, Canada M4V 3B2
Penguin Books (N.Z.) Ltd, 182–190 Wairau Road, Auckland 10, New Zealand

Penguin Books Ltd, Registered Offices: Harmondsworth, Middlesex, England

This edition published in 1992 by Viking Penguin, a division of Penguin Books USA Inc.

10   9   8   7   6   5   4   3   2   1

English text copyright © Rumer Godden, 1962
Copyright renewed Rumer Godden, 1990
Illustrations copyright © Bear Run Publishing, Inc., 1992
All rights reserved

The poems in this volume were selected from *Prayers from the Ark* by Carmen Bernos de Gasztold, translated from the French by Rumer Godden and published in 1962 by The Viking Press. The original French-language edition was published under the titles, *Le Mieux Aimé* and *Prières dans l'Arche*, 1947 and 1955 Copyright Editions du Cloitre.

Library of Congress Cataloging-in-Publication Data
Bernos de Gasztold, Carmen. [Prieres dans l'arche. English] Prayers from the ark /
[translated] by Rumer Godden : illustrated by Barry Moser   p.   cm.
Translation of: Prières dans l'arche / Carmen Bernos de Gasztold.
Summary: An illustrated collection of poems,
each a prayer by one of the animals in Noah's ark.

I S B N   0 - 6 7 0 - 8 4 4 9 6 - 9

1. Animals—Juvenile poetry.   2. Noah's ark—Juvenile poetry.
3. Children's poetry, French—Translations into English.
[1. Noah's ark—Poetry.   2. Animals—Poetry.   3. Prayers.   4. French
poetry.]   I. Godden, Rumer, 1907–   .   II. Moser, Barry, ill.   III. Title.
PQ2613.A655P7313   1992   841'.914—dc20   92–77   CIP   AC

Printed in U.S.A.
Set in 12 point Minion